Revolutionary Women

A Little Left of Center

Laura M. Duthie

Foreword

In conversations with people and/or when people have viewed my cartoons for the first time, they have often remarked; "Where are you coming from?" Well, to fill in a few of those blanks, here is a little of "where I'm coming from."

I was born in Toronto in 1957 to two Scottish immigrants. My parents came over in 1955 with my older sister. They had met in Gordon's School of Art. My father had just done his military service, and when he finished, he and my Mother tootled around Scotland on a motorcycle, got married and came to Canada. He is a fresh architect and she is a new mum.

I was born in Toronto Western and we lived on Oriole Parkway and then in a duplex on Mount Pleasant before my parents bought their first home in the suburbs of North Toronto. I have many memories of these places. I remember wanting to go to the park across the street and doing just that, with my tricycle. Only to find that this was not to my Mother's liking, as she was very upset to find her two-year-old daughter crossing a big city street like Eglinton Avenue West. I remember the night my Mother and Father told me I was big enough and didn't need to wear a diaper at night anymore. I also remember flying to Scotland around the same time, to visit my Mother's Mother. I remember the airplane ride, my Grandmother's house, and how horrible it was that they had left me there (for an afternoon) with this strange talking women who had knitted me a sweater. It was the only time I ever met my Grandmother. I remember struggling with my Mother and sister when they were trying to comb my hair and convince me to wear socks with my shoes and a dress for school.

I went to public school, junior high, and high school. I remember thinking at about four years old, just going into kindergarten, where little girls had to wear dresses and jeans were absolutely forbidden, what a big bore this school business was and that I would just have to wait until I was a "Big Girl" and out of school to do what I wanted to do.

The strap was still in use and teachers could hit you with books and slap you with rulers. In kindergarten, a great deal of my time was spent standing in the corner with a dunce hat on or displaying a piece of chewing gum on my nose. My grade one teacher was fond of lining up the "misbehaving children" at the front of the class and taking each one over her knee and giving them a few whacks with her ruler, myself included. She also used to tell me it was a sin to waste my artistic talent. Torture, humiliation, and convoluted encouragement, all the while being told to be seen and not heard. I also remember learning to read. The very first book I read was "Jack and Jill." I was totally disappointed at the role Jill played. Actually flat-out disappointed with what it meant to be a girl. I certainly didn't want to be her and was quite envious that Jack got to do all the fun active stuff with Spot. All she did was be a "good girl," wear a dress and stay at home with her mother.

For the most part, I hated school and didn't do tremendously well, although, I loved being able to do sports with other girls. By the time high school rolled around, I had resigned myself to getting better grades so I would be accepted by the college of my choice.

The idea of "more academics" and stringent rules didn't appeal to me, especially since I had some awareness about my own homosexuality and sought a more open-minded, liberal kind of place. Art school was the choice for me. Deep down inside, I hoped I might find some people just crazy enough to be gay.

Two years later, after three separate interviews, I finally got accepted at the Ontario College of Art. Dudley Gateskill, the ex-president of O.C.A. and a dear friend of our family, wrote me a letter of recommendation, he wished me luck in "keeping my own direction" once I got into art school. At the time, I remember thinking to myself, I know where I'm going, what did he mean by that?

I was 19 at the time. Well, Dudley knew what he was talking about, there were many paths to choose from. I remember the early days of walking down the halls, everyone seemed older and wore clothes that were very far out. Ripped paint-covered jeans, and straggling, unkempt hair were the norm. I'd found paradise.

There were the "commercial art" students, the texture photographers, the realists, the minimalists, the Jack Pollacks, the post impressionists, the transcendentalists, the Dadaists, the metallurgists welding "found scrap metal" together, the experimental artists (where a group of them would get together and with a huge canvas, lay it out in the middle of traffic and get cars to drive over it.) artists painting pain, others drawing beauty, perverted cartoonists, the drug artists, the drunken artists, some strung-out gay artists, a few middle class ladies and one blind fellow. All of us are struggling with the meaning of life and what was great art. I called myself a fine artist, and after a grueling first year, went into sculpture and bronze foundry. There were many talented and skilled students, I think I quickly came to the point of view that creating art and "Marking-it" were two completely different entities and one had nothing to do with the other. It was a time of high ideals and learning to deal with the opinions of others.

After art school, I went directly into commercial graphic arts, what a paradox, after studying fine arts, and thumbing my nose at the snotty commercial art students the whole time and then ending up in the slick world of advertising. Some friends said it was a betrayal of my values. On the contrary, it was like putting a polish on a rough stone. I stayed in graphics for about eight years until the economy turned down. It's an unfortunate human characteristic that the limb we are out on has to break before we make any attempt to save ourselves. At least that's how it was for me. So, on a bleak day in January of 1988, I was tired of being broke and vowed to get any kind of job. I changed jobs many times, got my real estate license, bought a house, expanded into property management, and worked at a job I hated. Shift work is the fastest way I know to get completely out of touch with yourself.

By about 1995, I had burned out and was completely overwhelmed by a steady diet of indigestible mind food. I was stuck in a "rut" and literally had to pull and drag myself away from that job to make the 180-degree career change back to myself and an artistic way of life.

The challenges and detours did not always seem (at the time) like welcome sources of character building, I wish there had been more support along the road. There are parts of my story that I haven't talked about like being brought-up by a brutal misogynist and being betrayed by the passive forbearance of my mother, of trying to commit suicide as a blossoming lesbian in adolescence, of becoming an alcoholic and amazingly recovering from it, oh and recovery from several different love relationships not to mention being passionately and deeply disenchanted by my fellow human beings with their harsh and sometimes cruel responses to their own difficulties and obstacles. Phobias galore.

I have discovered that when you hide who you really are, men and women feel betrayed somehow, that you hadn't been honest with them in the first place. To come out, to be able to laugh off the snipes, and smile gracefully when "breaking an assumption" of someone who has just pre-judged you, takes high self-esteem and steely courage not to flinch, hold your own ground, let them fling their opinions, and come back with kindness and an unwavering joy in being exactly who you are. There will be days your mother never told you about and situations where my father's macho bravado won't work, it'll make a situation worse. So, here's my "motus operand;" drain a grievance, laugh a little, heal a wound, and move on. If there's "crap" in your life, this is a great thing! Shine a light on it because it's valuable "crap." I know now, I must not shy away from the issues, situations, and people that bring me to my knees, trembling with fear, and sweating with self-doubt. Sometimes I still feel as if I'm four years old. This Feminist Book of Cartoons is a visual artist's journey through history, it's unique, often silly, sometimes serious point of view, but it's all me and I finally like who I am.

Dedication

"I would like to thank my parents Sandy & Gloria, and
my sisters Melisande & Eleanor and my best friend Gina,
for all their love and support."

Table of Contents

Revolutionary Women A Little Left of Center
Laura M. Duthie

Stonehenge

At around the same time, the Pyramids were being built, another pre-historic monument was being assembled. Archaeologists believe Stonehenge could be as old as 3000 B.C. As old if not older than, the Pyramids. Upon further investigations, they have found that the stones align with the sun at the summer and winter solstices, and serves as a giant calendar.

Today, it still has the ability to inspire us and to ask questions about its majesty and origin.

Was it a place of brutal sacrifice or sacred ritual? Was it built to honour Gods, or individuals going through a rite of passage? Was it a gathering place, where they exchanged stories or important news? Did they discuss or just listen? Was it solemn or did they celebrate with clever pageantry?

We don't know, but we do know from their burial sites that they were an egalitarian people because they placed all of the family members equally in the burial mounds. No one was more important than another.

Dare I say, is it not safe to assume Stonehenge was built not only by men but by men and women. Once again, the typical woman blind male historians have overlooked women's consistent contributions.

Revolutionary Women A Little Left of Center
Laura M. Duthie

Revolutionary Women A Little Left of Center
Laura M. Duthie

Revolutionary Women A Little Left of Center
Laura M. Duthie

Revolutionary Women A Little Left of Center
Laura M. Duthie

Revolutionary Women A Little Left of Center
Laura M. Duthie

Eve

The Holy Bible, what is it? A Sacred truth, an amazing piece of ancient literature, a collection of short stories, a newspaper with an editorial slant, partially true events blended with symbolic storytelling, a patriarchal manifesto, an arrogant dogma, designed to control large volumes of unruly people? Regardless of whether or not you believe in it or not, take it literally and devour it completely or just take little pieces, can you escape its influence"? A remarkable edict guarantying a place of importance for men. However, can we ever undo the damage it has done to women's lives and role as equal creators?

The Bible writers really "set the stage" in the first three pages of the Old Testament:

And God said: "I'm going to make me a man, in my likeness, and I'm going to let him have exclusive dominion over all the fish, birds, and cattle…and let him name them all (favoring) and then I'm going to make a garden with a trap in it, put Adam to gardening and…Oh, he'll need a "helper," so I'll take one of Adam's ribs, and make a woman, (Hence, one of the biggest lies known to womenkind is born; woman being created from a man. Aren't all men and women born of women?) And then the serpent from the "Tree of Knowledge" will say: "Eat this fruit, it will open your eyes," and gullible Eve will eat it and then offer it to Adam and he'll eat it too…" and then I will question them both and Adam will say Eve gave it to him, (A second Betrayal; He didn't have to eat it, basically blaming Eve) and Eve will believe she mislead everyone and will believe it's Eve fault because he listened to her and then I'll curse the snake and kick them out of the garden and men & women will be eternal enemies in holy matrimony forever and ever. And let them deal with the aftermath of being polarised. Eve will conceive in sorrow for her guilt and Adam can rule over Eve even though she is the mother of all living.

Revolutionary Women A Little Left of Center
Laura M. Duthie

Mary

On viewing and admiring, the many renditions of Jesus' Last Supper, a sacred and charged archetypal scene, I have always been dismayed, that at this last and important banquet, and with Jesus' Bible persona of an "All Loving Nature" that the story tellers and artists only saw to include one member of the opposite sex.

Who prepared the meal? Who served it? Who cleaned up? And where was Mary, and how did she feel about all of this? After all, Mary was the mother of the son of God. Wasn't she the one who had an "immaculate conception" and gave birth to a saviour?

She must have been pretty special to have enjoyed such an "intimate spiritual relationship" with God. But no mention of her, not even a salute to her contribution, even though she created the baby and the environment for the child to develop into an important influential person. Maybe she had something important to say.

Do we all collectively just take Mother for granted?

Revolutionary Women A Little Left of Center
Laura M. Duthie

Revolutionary Women A Little Left of Center
Laura M. Duthie

29

Revolutionary Women A Little Left of Center
Laura M. Duthie

Revolutionary Women A Little Left of Center
Laura M. Duthie

Sigmund Freud, 1856-1939

Sigmund Freud, known as the Father of Psychology, was revolutionary. He asked questions that no one wanted to ask, broke new ground in the area of human sexuality, opened up the mind and looked into the heart of human kind.

We have a lot to thank him for, especially for laying down a foundation from which to study human behavior in a Victorian era that prohibited exploration of human sexuality.

Unfortunately, we also inherited his female genitalia blind perspective. He was true to himself and true to his own sex, maybe, but clearly lacked a female perspective. Everything was sexual to him and all problems related back to repressed infantile sexual aggression and physical endowment. Aggression and erections are all very interesting, but what has it got to do with bleeding and birthing? How could he know first-hand about the uterus or vagina when his unique perspective from the penis limited him?

He really clouded our view of the female species when he said, "In the phallic/clitoris phase of childhood development after the third year, when boys and girls first discover their genitals are different, they develop a fear of female genitalia and envy of male genitalia. You'd have to be a woman to know that women don't want to be men. Women like being women. I think the sight of his own penis overwhelmed him so much that he couldn't see anything else.

Let's flip the equation and write it from a female perspective and just call it male narcissism/powerlessness versus womb envy.

He also prescribed and experimented with cocaine on his patients and himself. Cocaine was the active ingredient in Coca-Cola in the 1920's so one might easily conclude he had a few hang-ups of his own.

Revolutionary Women A Little Left of Center
Laura M. Duthie

Meet the Phobe Family

Meet the Phobe Family...that's Phobe as in Phobia or Phobic. A Phobia is a little different then just plain fear, and I'm not talking about a healthy fear of imminent danger. I'm talking about an irrational, persistent and imagined fear of people, places or situations! These folks are stuck in a world of paralysing beliefs and superstitions. Now, imagine struggling and searching to find someone special enough to bring home to mother...when you realise you've just walked into a Phobe Family!

Revolutionary Women A Little Left of Center
Laura M. Duthie

Revolutionary Women A Little Left of Center
Laura M. Duthie

Revolutionary Women A Little Left of Center
Laura M. Duthie

Revolutionary Women A Little Left of Center
Laura M. Duthie

Revolutionary Women A Little Left of Center
Laura M. Duthie

Revolutionary Women A Little Left of Center
Laura M. Duthie

Copyright Laura M. Duthie 2007

#07090

Revolutionary Women A Little Left of Center
Laura M. Duthie

Copyright Laura M. Duthie 2007   #07092

Revolutionary Women A Little Left of Center
Laura M. Duthie

Revolutionary Women A Little Left of Center
Laura M. Duthie

Revolutionary Women A Little Left of Center
Laura M. Duthie

Copyright Laura M. Duthie 2010　　　　#10095

Revolutionary Women A Little Left of Center
Laura M. Duthie

Revolutionary Women A Little Left of Center
Laura M. Duthie

Revolutionary Women A Little Left of Center
Laura M. Duthie

Revolutionary Women A Little Left of Center
Laura M. Duthie

Revolutionary Women A Little Left of Center
Laura M. Duthie

Revolutionary Women A Little Left of Center
Laura M. Duthie

www.ingramcontent.com/pod-product-compliance
Lightning Source LLC
Chambersburg PA
CBHW041143300726
48978CB00016B/1359